TWISTAPLOT

12

JOURNEY TO VERNICO 5

Megan Stine and
H. William Stine

Illustrations by Robert Roper

SCHOLASTIC INC.
New York Toronto London Auckland Sydney Tokyo

For Anne Stine—who yearns to travel

ISBN 0-590-33213-9

12 11 10 9 8 7 6 5 4 3 2   4 5 6 7 8 9/8
Printed in the U.S.A.   01

BEWARE!!!
DO NOT READ THIS BOOK FROM BEGINNING TO END

It is the year 2113 and you are about to leave your home planet for an accidental journey through time and space to the remote and unexpected world of Vernico 5.

Something is very wrong on Vernico 5, and you have stumbled onto its secret. If you make the right choices you may be able to save the entire galaxy from a madman's terrible control. The wrong decisions, however, can lead to intergalactic chaos and even your own untimely death.

So be careful, future traveler, as you step into the distant darkness known as Space. The stars are beautiful all around you, but they burn exceedingly hot. Wise visitors understand the planets are their only friends.

Now climb aboard the capsule that will take you on an unforgettable journey — the Journey to Vernico 5!

Rockets are zipping past your head, firing lethal dropons at you. The noise is almost deafening. But still your hands are steady on the controls. Slowly you push the firing button and blow up one Zorga rocket after another. Hey, you're really getting your four dollars' worth out of this 3-D Zorga Avengers vid-screen game! Look at the score you're racking up. Whoops — the Tarnoid attack just turned your best fleet scooter into space dust.

But you keep playing, because you know that when the game stops, your Aunt Doro can break in on screen and tell you it's time to practice your laser piano lessons. If she finds you, she won't think twice about sending out the Fourth Unit robot to drag you home.

As soon as you begin to hear Aunt Doro's voice, you run outside. Practice piano? No way!!! You've got to find a place to hide. There's a cargo unit being loaded into a space freighter. And the data nord on your wrist tells you the freighter won't lift off until it has 82 cargo units on board. So you leap onto it and sigh with relief.

Five seconds later, the space freighter takes off.

Oh, well, Aunt Doro, you say to yourself, *see you sometime . . . I hope.*

Go on to PAGE 4.

4

...he space freighter blasts into light-speed, and you pass out. When you come to, it takes a while for you to remember where you are and how you got there. Then you hear a computerized announcement: *Northsat coordinate EDT 19.7. Underhold deployment. Destination: Vernico 5.*

You don't understand most of that. But you have heard of Vernico 5. It's a newly colonized planet, probably pretty primitive. It's populated with a bunch of rejects — people who don't officially exist because they went bankrupt or lost their data nords or couldn't pass the mandatory Standards/Understanding Test. In other words, you wouldn't send your worst enemy to a reject colony — and you certainly don't want to end up there yourself!

But what choice do you have? Suddenly you see a button marked JETTISON ESCAPE CAPSULE. You push it and a hatch opens, revealing a small escape capsule. Small? It's tiny — no bigger than a trisatellite callbooth! What should you do?

If you're a daredevil, hop in the escape capsule and turn to PAGE 12.

If you're not a daredevil, stay on the space freighter to Vernico 5 and turn to PAGE 14.

You give Rory your data nord, and he walks away. You wait for him to return, and your mind changes as regularly as the clock. *He'll be back any minute . . . maybe something went wrong . . . maybe Dr. Enutelle caught him . . . why am I kidding myself — it was a trick . . . Rory stole my data nord and now I'm a reject — forever . . .*

These are your thoughts as you fight off sleep. But finally the door slides open.

"You're wanted by the police," Rory whispers, handing back your data nord. "What did you do, anyway?"

"Skipped my piano lesson," you say, but it's not funny, even to you, anymore. "How'd your call go?"

"My family was surprised, and really happy. They told me to do anything I could to help you. I know where you can hide. But we've got to move right now while it's dark," Rory says.

"Or I can find out what's going on in that S.T. Substation and then send a message to the Intergalactic Council. If I have proof, they'll come and protect me," you say.

"It's up to you, but you don't have a minute to waste," Rory says.

If you want to go to the substation and investigate, turn to PAGE 22.

If you want to hide, turn to PAGE 30.

6

You really know how to hurt a droyfer, don't you — and just in time, too. You run out of the room. Forget the elevator without buttons — that's not going to get you anywhere. How about a good old-fashioned window to jump out of? It's about the only thing you haven't done today. Just to make sure everything will go smoothly, you throw a chair through the window first. The chair breaks the glass and sets off an alarm. But you're down the road before anyone knows what happened.

You slow down when you come to a crowd of rejects standing around a dwelling module. They are moaning and banging their heads together in an ancient and outlawed mourning ritual. You squeeze into the crowd. It's a good place to hide — and besides, curiosity is overwhelming you.

In the dwelling, a young reject's body lies on the floor. She is twisted and green and rock-solid. Her face clearly shows her final moments were painful.

"She killed herself," one of the rejects says to you. Strangely, the rejects are not afraid or cautious about talking to you. They show you the note she wrote: *Better no breath than a slave's breath.*

"The Treatment has killed her," someone says through his tears.

Go on to PAGE 66.

The reject takes you to his dwelling module, a two-room, one-story house — one of the many one-window houses at the far edge of the colony.

He brings out a clay bowl with fruit in it. The pieces of fruit look as small as gumdrops in his huge hands.

"I have a reputation for being old-fashioned," he explains. "Rejects build their own dwelling modules, and some use low-power tools. Not me. I like to do everything with my hands." As he speaks, he picks up an orangeapple in his massive fist and rubs it on his shirt to polish it. Then he begins to slowly peel off the skin. "Most people use a knife to do this. Not me," he says. His eyes never leave your eyes to look at the fruit as he carefully strips away the rind without piercing the fruit. "Take killing someone. Most people rush out and buy some fancy, newfangled weapon — laser splatter, a cathode knife, fusion impactor. Not me." He pops the orangeapple into his mouth — whole. Then, in a flash, he grabs you and begins to squeeze your neck with his huge, rough hands.

Go on to PAGE 8.

You kick, you squirm, you flail your arms; but he doesn't seem to feel any of it as he lifts you into the air until your eyes are level with his.

"Dr. Enutelle doesn't like to take any chances," he says. "He's old-fashioned, too."

You can't break his hold on you, and you can barely breathe. With fear opening your eyes wide, you grab his head and pull yourself close to him. Closer — your face is almost resting against the side of his. Then you scream a scream you never dreamed was in you, right into his ear! He drops you and grabs his head, shaking and holding his ears. But he's only momentarily stunned. Quickly you pick up a log by the fireplace and bring it down on his foot as fast as you can. You swing it again, this time at both of his shins. He howls as he tries to limp toward you.

"I guess I'm pretty old-fashioned myself," you say as you run out of the dwelling module at top speed.

If you'd give anything to see a familiar face right now, turn to PAGE 52.

If you'd rather meet a real reject, turn to PAGE 28.

You remain a Willingness Worker and one of the best, too, for whatever that's worth. You beg like a dog, pour acid on artwork, and drag people by their toes whenever you're told to do it. But at least you kept your integrity — you didn't allow them to erase your memory.

Eventually Enutelle rewards your good work by allowing you to be the one to push the button that turns everyone in the universe into Willingness Workers.

Close the book now before we twist your ears off.

THE END

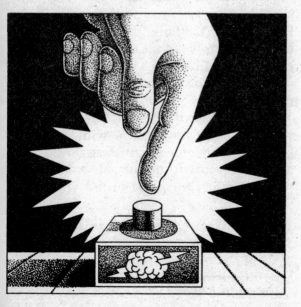

You can run very fast on Vernico because of the low gravity, so you catch up with the governor in an instant. The words tumble out of you. You hope you're making sense.

"Governor Slone, you've got to do something. I got on a space freighter by mistake and came to Vernico and guards kidnapped me because of what they picked up on a TCR and then they gassed me and General Bartus split me in half and interrogated me but I didn't know anything so he let me go . . . but listen to this: I saw *Dr. Enutelle* on Vernico 5 this morning!"

The governor puts his hand on your shoulder and leads you off to the side. "We know about Enutelle," he tells you quietly. "In fact, we're on Vernico to investigate why that madman is here."

"What's going on here? A reject just told me Vernico has a terrible secret," you say.

"It's not a terrible secret, but it is a top secret," the governor says with a smile. "You've seen enough to deserve an answer. But you will not be able to repeat a word of what I'm going to tell you now, understand?"

Of course you don't, yet. But you will soon.

Go on to PAGE 11.

"You've probably noticed that Vernico does not look like a typical reject colony. Such colonies are primitive, built by the rejects' own hands. This one is modern," the governor says.

"And it has an enormous Science Transport Substation," you add.

"Yes, the government built that substation here for Professor Bashi Dworkin, so that he could perfect his Nonmaterial Transportation System," Slone explains.

"His what??" you ask.

"I told you it was top secret. Professor Dworkin is developing a transportation system between planets that won't require a spaceship. In other words, one minute you're on Vernico 5, the next minute you're back home on Nector Alpha," Slone says.

"I could use that right now," you say.

"Sounds like you've had a full morning," he says with a smile. "But you did the right thing in coming to me. Tell me where all of this happened, and I'll personally investigate it."

You sigh with relief and give the governor every detail. Then he arranges special T2 clearance for you to captain a one-person space rambler home.

If you want to go home, turn to PAGE 64.
If not, turn to PAGE 24.

You squeeze into the escape capsule and hit the GO button. The floor under the capsule drops open, and two nitro-fero rockets blast you away from the freighter. After burnout, you coast for a while and then flip on your homing signal. It won't be long now before a ship rescues you.

What's there to snack on? you wonder. As you turn around in the snug-fitting capsule, your elbow accidentally bumps a button marked DO NOT PUSH THIS BUTTON. Suddenly a rocket fires, and the capsule takes off like a blast from a gun. When you finally come to a stop, you have no idea where in the galaxy you are. And the only sound is the beep of your homing signal.

But instantly, a giant spaceship is hovering over you and pulling you into its open port. There's only one problem: You've never seen a ship like this in your district before. And since there are no Intergalactic Council code markings, you're pretty sure this is not a rescue ship!

Go on to PAGE 88.

"You're not a flashlight! You're a human being!" a policeman yells, trying to snap you out of it.

"Don't say that," another policeman says. "I'm still writing my report and I need the extra light."

"Listen to me," the first policeman says, shaking you a little. "You have survived the silent dome and we now believe you are innocent. But we need your help in capturing the leaders of this black market."

You're still pretty groggy, but finally you ask, "What do you want me to do?"

"We want you to deliver the shipment to your planned destination," the police tell you. "What do you say?"

"I'll need backup support," you say.

"We'll be in a spaceship right behind you," they say.

"I'll need to call my aunt and tell her where I am," you say.

"You can go to space-com immediately," they say.

"And I'll need a new bulb and plenty of D-batteries," you say.

"Uh-oh," they say. "Maybe you need to get a little more rest first."

If you think you can make the delivery by yourself, go to PAGE 21.

If you want a robot partner, go to PAGE 27.

The landing on Vernico 5 is smooth, but looking around gives you a strange feeling. Something about the colony doesn't add up. There are too many people and too many dwelling/working modules. It definitely doesn't look like other reject colonies you've seen on the vid-tube.

"When was all of this built?" you ask at a food module.

"Well, I'm pretty new here, but people say most of this was started in 2107," the food tech tells you.

How can this be? You know it takes 15 years to build a complete Science Transport Substation. And the Vernico substatation across the street is the largest, most up-to-date you've ever seen.

You start subtracting — 2107 from 2113 — that's only six years. Six years to build Vernico? Impossible. Someone's got to be lying.

Suddenly down the street, you see a lot of faces you recognize — faces you've seen on the vid-tube. They are famous scientists, governors, and leaders of the defense council. Even the governor of your district, Ian Slone, is there. What are they doing here? People like them wouldn't normally visit a reject colony, not even on a bet!

Go on to PAGE 15.

Across the street from the politicans and scientists, you see another familiar face. And he's the last person in the galaxy you'd ever want to meet — Dr. Glaret Enutelle. People say that he has invented a mind control plan that could turn the entire galaxy into a bunch of mindless Nodz!

As you watch, Dr. Enutelle disappears around a corner in the flat, gray city and down one of the narrow little walkways, which is crowded because transportation is banned on reject colonies. You look at the huge Science Transport Substation on one side of the main walkway, and all of the little one-room buildings on the other side and try to figure it out. Who built all this? Without modern tools and supplies, the rejects couldn't have done it.

Just then you see the group of governors, including Ian Slone, coming toward the launch site, and boarding their individual diplomatic shuttle ships.

Now's your chance to get some answers — maybe.

If you want to ask Ian Slone what's going on here, turn to PAGE 35.

If you just want to follow Enutelle and snoop around on your own, turn to PAGE 59.

"Look!" Clare shouts, pointing to the word you wrote. "I told you he was human inside. Don't you see? We can't kill these beasts. We've got to help them."

"A charming speech, my dear," Dr. Enutelle says, bursting into the lab with some of his guards. "I'm sure I will remember that speech long after the sweet memory of your screams of pain and agony has faded from my mind." Then he turns to his guards and snaps, "Kill her immediately!"

If you want to use your animal strength, instinct, and teeth to maul him to death, turn to PAGE 73.

If you want to retain as much of your humanity as possible, resist that impulse and turn to PAGE 45.

"Just try to rule the universe and I'll turn your ribcage into an accordion," you say, enjoying this feeling of power more than you should.

"No Problem," Slone says. "Don't hurt me. I'll do anything."

"Okay — first tell me who else is in on this with you? The other governors?"

"No. No one. They only came here to find out why Enutelle was here. I came to help him obscure his true purpose."

"All right. Now you'd better find a way to turn off your friend Enutelle or we'll relocate your armpits," you say.

"No Problem. Only there is a problem with that. There's *no way* to turn off Enutelle. Better let me try to turn off his bomb instead. I think I've seen enough to know how to defuse it. Want me to give it a try?"

If you want to let Slone try to defuse the bomb, turn to PAGE 49.

If you'd rather go to the other governors and let them deal with Enutelle, turn to PAGE 78.

"I can't lend you my data nord," you say. "If you lost it, I'd be a reject."

"I'll bring it back. Don't you believe me?"

"I believe you, but it's against the law for me to take it off," you say.

"I'll take it off for you," Rory says, with new anger in his voice. He takes a cord out of his pocket, spins it in the air twice, and suddenly it glows fire-hot. "I'll take your whole hand off," he says.

You quickly press a key on your data nord. "Now you'll have to kill me to take it off, Rory. Are you prepared to do that?"

He closes the space between the two of you, one slow step at a time.

"Back off, Rory. We don't need to see any more," says a voice over a hidden speaker.

Just then Ian Slone and the other governors burst in.

"Your aunt was right about you," Slone says. "You're just the kind of kid we need for a special mission. Sorry about having to put you through this kind of an S.U. Test, but we had to be sure."

Twenty-four hours later, you are on your way to a vast, unexplored galaxy. By the time you arrive, you're 25 years old, and you have become the respected Peace Ambassador from your home galaxy. The salary is beyond your wildest dreams!

THE END

What planet have you been living on, ace? Hitting a droyfer in the foolip (#2) and the inner tumkis (#3) is a self-defensive move about on the same par as telling him his shoelaces are untied.

He drags you to the front of the line by your index fingers, then puts the smooth, eyeless, steel mask over your head. You hear a buzz; you see the mask glow. But you don't feel any different.

The next thing you know, the droyfer lets you go free!

You wander the building for a while, trying to get out; but every time you near an exit, someone threatens you and you hear yourself say, "No Problem." Then you back off.

Finally you open the door to a room on the 23rd floor that should be familiar to you, but you don't have the slightest memory of it. Rejects are standing in a line, waiting for a droyfer to squeeze a stainless steel, eyeless mask over their heads. You don't know what this treatment is, but you have a feeling it isn't a beauty treatment!

"Stop it!" you shout, bursting into the room. "Why are you people letting them do this to you?"

Go on to PAGE 36.

You're flying the spaceship over a desert and toward a mountain. This is where the navigation computer says the black market delivery is to be made. Before you climb out of the spaceship, you check in with the police again.

"We're right behind you," they say, although they're nowhere in sight. "Just get the guy to talk about what he does with the stuff and who sends it to him. If there's trouble, just shout into your throat-com."

A minute later you are standing in front of the ID camera outside a large, all Plexiglas house.

"I have a shipment for you," you say.

By the time you bring in all of the cargo units, a man has appeared at the door.

"What do you want with all this stuff?" you ask, trying to sound casual.

Instead of answering, the man asks you a question. "How do you know what's in here? You were instructed not to look."

The man suddenly pushes you inside and seals the front door. "Sometimes what you do know can hurt you," the man says. He pulls out a torque knife from inside his stomach and pushes you toward the interior of his house. "You can scream as loud and as long as you want. No one will be able to hear you in here," he warns.

Go on to PAGE 54.

"How do I get into the S.T. Substation?" you ask Rory.

But Rory doesn't get a chance to answer, because instantly a woman starts pounding on the door and shouting, "Substation security guard! Open up, reject!"

Rory pushes you toward his sleeping alcove. "Go in there and hide behind a light panel. I'll think of something," he says.

He opens the front door just before the guard pushes it in. You listen to everything from the alcove.

"Where is the illegal visitor? Thermal sensors indicate the visitor is here."

"Gone. The visitor is gone," Rory says.

"Gone? Where has the visitor gone?" she shouts.

"I don't know," Rory says.

And you begin to breathe again.

"Reject, if I have to use my sabatin on you, your bones will snap like pencils," the woman says.

"No Problem. The visitor is hiding behind a light panel in my sleeping alcove," Rory says in a voice that's not his own.

"Thanks. I love you Willingness Workers. You make my job so easy."

As the woman stomps toward your hiding place, you imagine the sound of pencils snapping.

Go on to PAGE 91.

Turning this garbage into space trash is against the law, but it's the only way you can think of to get rid of it once and for all. So you program a robot to carry all the drums to the dumper hatch. Then you push the EJECT button, but nothing happens. The chute is probably jammed, you decide. You have to climb in to inspect the hatch, hoping that it doesn't fix itself while you're in there. You climb out quickly and try the button again. Nothing doing. What's going on?

Suddenly a voice breaks into your spaceship's space-com system. *This is the police. Do not attempt to remove any of the evidence. We have electronically sealed your craft. You cannot escape,* says the mechanical voice.

Two minutes later, your spaceship is bursting with Intergalactic Council police and police robots. Two of the robots lift you off the ground and hold you there, while other police officers go through the drums in the dumper hatch.

Then a police robot captain wheels over to you and says, *You're under arrest for smuggling and trafficking in illegal merchandise. I'm going to make sure you stay in jail until you rust.*

Go on to PAGE 47.

The T2 clearance has come through, and you're climbing on board the space rambler when you see Glinton Canarr. Glinton used to live near you in your full-time unit. He's standing in a small crowd, staring at all the diplomatic ships on their launch-pads. You jump down and push through the crowd to get to Glinton.

"Glinton, what are *you* doing here?" you ask.

Glinton is just as surprised to see you as you are to see him. The two of you smack the backs of your hands in greeting.

"Do you remember that guy Keddy Bloom?" Glinton asks.

"I could forget Keddy Bloom about as easily as I could forget a blister on my tongue." you say.

"Well, he flunked his S.U. Test and he knew it. So before he left the tester terminal, he input my test so it looked as if I flunked, too. They took my data nord, called me a reject, and sent me here," Glinton says. "Can you believe it?"

You just stare into Glinton's desperate eyes for a minute. It's so awful, there's nothing you can say.

"But, let me tell you something," Glinton goes on. "That's nothing compared to what's happening on Vernico 5."

Go on to PAGE 25.

"What *is* going on here?" you ask Glinton.

"Dr. Enutelle is turning rejects into Willingness Workers," Glinton says, lowering his voice. "Do you remember the Nodz from fifty years ago?"

"Sure, someone invented a serum to turn people into zombies — mental zeros," you say softly.

"Well, Enutelle has a new Treatment that does the same thing — only worse. You feel exactly like yourself after it — think your own thoughts and everything. But you'll do anything anyone tells you to do. All they have to do is threaten to hurt you and you hear yourself saying, 'No Problem.'"

"How do you know about it?" you ask.

"They're asking rejects to volunteer for the Treatment, promising their reject status will be changed," Glinton says. "But it's a lie. And I don't know *what* they do if you refuse the Treatment. It's going to be my turn soon."

"No, it won't, Glinton," you say, pushing your friend. "Get into this space rambler. You're blasting off this planet."

If you want to leave Vernico with Glinton, turn to PAGE 83.

If you want to stay and tell Governor Slone about the Treatment, turn to PAGE 46.

There is a window across from you. Outside you can see a lush, tropical land. Thick purple trees sway in the wind blowing off a yellow ocean. This planet, whatever and wherever it is, is one of the most beautiful you've ever seen.

But when you turn around and look at the thing that's in the small cage with you, the planet takes on a terrifying image.

The animal has an apelike face and a head with thick, tufted fur on its nose. Its long green arms are scaly, and its thin legs have two toes.

A door opens and lights come on. Your cage is in some kind of laboratory. A young woman enters and puts on a white lab coat.

"Let's get right to business," she says, throwing scraps of something into the cage, which the beast gobbles quickly. "The planet you're on is called Nova Cruz. It is an unknown planet belonging to Dr. Enutelle, who uses it to further his scientific understanding. Your roommate is called an Amprodusian. Dr. Enutelle would like you to choose whether you want to be an Amprodusian or undergo a human head graft. You have 10 seconds to decide."

If you think you'd do better as an Amprodusian, turn to PAGE 41.

If you'd rather be a two-headed human, turn to PAGE 53.

"If the customer asks, you came along to do the heavy work," you tell the police robot partner that has been assigned to you.

Don't worry. I don't think the customer will ask anything about me, the robot replies.

The delivery coordinates in the navigation computer bring you to a house on a mountaintop on the planet Gemini.

A kindly old woman answers the door, and with a surprised look at the robot, says, "Oh. I didn't expect to see you."

"I'm the new deliveryperson," you say.

"Gravestock is hiring them young these days, isn't he?" she says.

"So *that's* the name of the man who sent me!" you say.

"My, my. You mean you don't even know the name of the man who is responsible for ordering your death?" she says. "Grab the little idiot, Roger."

Turn to PAGE 93.

Maybe you should have smacked *both* of his feet when you had the chance, you think as you race out of the dwelling module. Even limping, the tall assassin is giving you a good run for your life. You're in the streets in a flash, but you're flat on your face in another instant. You try to stand up, but you slip again, bracing your fall with your arms. While you were inside, there was an oil storm. Now the streets and artificial ground of Vernico are slick, and your shoes won't give you any traction.

You practically rip your feet off removing your shoes as fast as you can. Then you take off again down the street. There's no need to look back — you know who's back there. But what's ahead? If you can just find someplace to hide, or maybe *someone* to hide you.

You skid to a stop in front of a young man with long blond hair who's sitting on a bench looking up at Vernico's triangular suns.

"Help me," you say. "Don't let him catch me."

Go on to PAGE 29.

The young man throws his coat around you just as the assassin goes hobbling by. When the street is clear, the young man takes you to hide in his dwelling module. It's a small gray room with one small table and a chair.

"Thanks," you say. "What's your name?"

"Rejects aren't allowed to have names," he says. "But I used to be called Rory. That seems like a long time ago. They sent me here two years ago for not having my data nord."

You immediately touch the silicon card that slides into an electronic slot on your wrist.

"They said I lost it. And I wasn't fit to live among responsible people. But I didn't lose it. I threw it away!"

"Threw it away??" you say. "But with a data nord you can know everything about anything in the galaxy. Without one, you don't exist!"

"I didn't want to know everything. I just wanted to be left alone," Rory says. "I had no idea what *alone* meant until I got to Vernico 5."

"What's going on here?" you ask. "Why doesn't this look like every other reject colony?"

"Because it's *not*," Rory says.

Go on to PAGE 40.

You think about it for a picon and a half, and then say to Rory, "Let's travel." Sneaking out in the darkness, the two of you walk to a place on the other side of Vernico, a side where one triangular sun casts a beautiful dim glow and never sets. A small colony of rejects have started a new world there. Their first project was to dig a hole for an artificial lagoon into Vernico's ugly surface, and when you and Rory arrive, you take a swim.

Dwellings are dug into mountainsides, and warmth comes from campfires. Here you live out the rest of your life without fear of the Vernico rulers or the substation guards, who don't know — and never find out — that this colony exists.

THE END

When the guard returns to his table, his food is cold and his jacket is missing.

Outside, you slip the jacket on. But it's almost as though it's alive, as though it knows you're not its real owner. The jacket tries to squeeze you around the chest and push your arms out of the sleeves.

But you get it on in time to pass the guards at the Science Transport Substation.

Being inside the building is like being on another planet. Everything is brightly lit, plants and vivid colors flourish, and air carts carry people from one area to another.

Suddenly a finger taps your shoulder. "Hey — are you Trag? We've been looking all over for you," a voice says. You turn to face another guard in a black jacket. "Next time you take a dinner break, Trag, let someone know where you're going. We didn't know where to find you."

"Sorry," you say in a voice you hope sounds like Trag's. "What's up?"

"Professor Dworkin wants to see you immediately — sounds important," says the guard. "Sixth floor, Room 65."

Go on to PAGE 48.

Your animal instincts tell you exactly the right instant to spring at the boy with the syringe. You swing your scaly arms and kick him with your spiny toes. The boy jumps back in pained surprise. You don't want to, but your will to survive is driving you to kill him now before he kills you and the other Amprodusian.

Suddenly you feel a sting in your side. You turn and see that Clare has shot you with a lab tech's dart gun. Your legs slip from under you, and you die quickly and painlessly.

The escaped young rebels continue their night raids on Enutelle's labs until all of the captives waiting their fates in cages are freed and all of the cruel experiments destroyed. They create a true Utopia on the planet Nova Cruz. And the evil Enutelle never returns.

THE END

When the guard returns to his table, you are sitting in his chair, finishing his meal. "Be with you in a second," you say. "Hate to be interrogated on an empty stomach."

The guard ID's you on his data nord and then drags you off to the Science Transport Substation.

"I guess I just got too close to the secret of Phase 2 of the Willingness Workers," you say as you walk. You have no idea what you're talking about, but just maybe you can bluff him and pick up some information.

"Phase 2?" the guard asks. "What does he need Phase 2 for after he launches that missile?"

"Missile?? Umm, well, he's not going to launch it," you say.

"He's not? But how else can he turn everyone in the universe into Willingness Workers? I like Willingness Workers. I just have to talk loud to them and they'll do whatever I say," the guard says with a big smile.

It's worked! Now you know what Dr. Enutelle is up to! But what can you do about it?

If you feel like giving Enutelle a piece of your mind right now, turn to PAGE 60.

If you'd rather try to outsmart him, go to PAGE 69.

"I thought you'd provide the transportation," you say, walking around the sealed drums.

"Me?! What's next? You want fringe benefits and a company picnic?" His laugh rings through the cargo hold of his ship. But it shuts off fast. "I ought to blast you back into space without your capsule for wasting my time, kid."

All of a sudden things aren't going your way, and you start to sweat. "How about this?" you say quickly. "You take my capsule. I'll take *this* ship, make the delivery, and meet you next week just as we planned."

He smiles and gives your face a small slap again. "The meeting coordinates for next week are in the navigation computer. You be there next week, or you'll be nowhere the week after. Got it?"

With that friendly reminder, he leaves in your escape capsule. You wander the ship for half an hour before you can even find the navigation chamber. Finally you do, and you sit down at the controls.

If you're over 16, you already have your space vehicle license, so go on to PAGE 65.

If you're under 16, turn to PAGE 74 for your learner's permit exam.

Just as you reach the group of governor's aides surrounding Ian Slone, a buzzer and warning light go off. Uh-oh . . . you must have been standing near a thought control receptor (TCR). In seconds, you are swooped up by police guards in shiny black vylar uniforms. They drag you to a large concrete building — the only other multi-room building you can see on the planet aside from the S.T. Substation. They throw you into a room with no windows and a very low ceiling. When you stand up, you hit your head and fall to the floor unconscious.

The next time you open your eyes, you are tied up, sitting in a chair in a different room. But the room is hard to see because it's filling up with a blue gas. You check the data nord on your wrist. The news isn't good. It says you've got 3.5 minutes to live.

Your mind grows fuzzy, and you start to pass out again. A million questions are spinning in your head: What's going on on Vernico? Why have you been arrested? And why are all those big shots here — including Ian Slone? Will you ever get out of here alive?

Go to PAGE 43.

One reject answers you. "They'll change my reject status — I'll get to go home."

"You fool! Don't do it. It's a trick!" you cry.

"Why don't you come over here and help us apply the mask," says one of the droyfers.

"Forget it," you sneer. "I don't get my kicks by being cruel."

"Do it *now* or I'll crush your shoulder set!" the droyfer says without even raising an arm in your direction.

A nauseous feeling sweeps over you.

"No Problem," you say. You step forward and begin fitting the mask on the rejects in front of you.

When you've done 70 rejects, Slone and Enutelle burst into the room.

"Here is the intruder, our newest Willingness Worker. I thought you'd be pleased," Governor Slone explains.

"Idiot!" shouts Enutelle. "Someone from Nector Alpha is bound to come looking for him, and the one thing I don't need is more visitors. I gave you your instructions: memory erasure and then propelled home — and that's what I meant!!"

If you want to have your memory of the past week erased, turn to PAGE 61.

If that's a fate worse than death to you, turn to PAGE 9.

You take the minisyringe and slowly raise it toward the neck of the krolt.

But amazingly, your hand holding the needle snaps up — and sticks you in your own neck! Apparently, the krolt's will was strong enough to dominate and control your arm. You die, but the krolt lives on — in your body.

The krolt is uncontrollable. He leaves the lab and terrorizes the planet. He commits unimaginable atrocities that are so awful you wouldn't even want to hear about them ... so we won't tell you.

THE END

"I forgot something in my space capsule," you say.

"Yeah? What did you forget?" the man asks, putting his face close to yours.

"I forgot to stay in it, you slime," you say, shifting your legs into high gear.

But the man doesn't come after you. Instead he opens a cargo cabinet and lets out a small robot. The robot has jaws and teeth on every part of its head. The man uses a long pole to switch it on. The robot comes to life and immediately snaps the pole to toothpicks with its teeth. Then it starts to look for you.

You've seen this kind of robot before. It's a robot watchdog, called Man's Worst Friend. It's programmed to attack everyone — even its own master!

The man is hidden on the other side of the room. The robot hasn't found you yet, but you fake a scream of pain. You hear the man start to laugh harder and harder, until his laughter cuts off with a gulp. "Not me, you stupid machine," he shouts. "Beat it before I strip your gears! *Ahhhrgg!*"

He's going to be busy for a while, so you take the opportunity to climb back into the space capsule and jettison out again. But right before you go to lightspeed, you see something outside you can't believe.

Go on to PAGE 90.

Rory lowers his voice even more. "Something horrible is going on in that Science Transport Substation. You should have seen the way they built it. They brought it up almost all put together! And then they orbited the pieces around Vernico and brought them down one by one. They were in a big hurry for some reason," he says.

"What's going on in there?" you ask.

"I don't know. Rejects aren't allowed in. Professor Bashi Dworkin is supposed to be working on some kind of a top secret project. But no one has seen him come out of the S.T. Substation in months," Rory says.

"What about Dr. Enutelle?" you ask.

"He's here most of the time. But this is the first time all those politicians have been here. I don't know what they're doing, really. What do you think?"

You haven't made up your mind yet, and before you can decide, Rory changes the subject. "Now I've got a favor to ask you. Let me borrow your data nord — just for an hour. If I have one I can walk into a space-com center and make a trisatellite call to my family. It's been years since I've seen them. This might be my only chance."

If you're willing to lend your data nord to Rory, turn to PAGE 5.

If you're not, turn to PAGE 19.

The procedure is a success. When it is over, you are the perfect likeness of that horrible creature in your cage.

When you are thrown back in the cage, the Amprodusian runs to a corner at first. He screams at you, and you find yourself screaming at him from the opposite corner.

Then he begins a dance to determine supremacy. His arms swing menacingly at you, and for some reason you do the same thing — you swing your long, skinny arms back and forth in front of his face. The part of you that's still human understands this territorial ritual, but the part of you that's Amprodusian just wants first crack at the pile of food. Finally, because your arms are longer than his, your scales catch him on the side of the face, and he retreats.

The food scraps are yours. You scarf down every last bite. Then you sleep peacefully — until the middle of the night. That's when you hear human voices outside.

Go on to PAGE 42.

Two young people enter the lab, close the door, and turn on the lights.

"Here are two more of Enutelle's experiments. We've got to kill them," says a boy.

"I still think it's wrong," a girl says. "These creatures were people once, until Enutelle got his hands on them. I'm sure we can find a way to reverse the procedure."

"Grow up, Clare," the boy says, finding a hypodermic needle and a bottle of some kind of liquid in the lab. "You've been on Nova Cruz long enough to know that most of these experiments are irreversible. Look what happened to most of our friends. Now we've finally gotten free. We've got to wipe out all the results of that fiend's work."

"I know," she says, looking into your cage and smiling sadly.

"And don't forget what they did to your hand, Clare," the boy says.

"How can I forget?" Clare says, holding up her left hand. On the end, instead of a hand, there is a small animal's head. It seems to be alive!

Then the boy opens your cage door. "Let's get this over with," he says, pointing the syringe at you.

If you want to attack him, turn to PAGE 32.

If you want to trick them, turn to PAGE 87.

You wake up in a third room, this one octagonal with walls of glass.

"Yes, you are still alive," a voice says from behind you. Someone walks slowly around to face you. His rough blue skin and the red teeth in his speech hole tell you two things about him immediately: He's a crayt, and you don't want to make him angry. "My name is General Bartus. That is a name you'll remember the rest of your life. How long you live depends on what you tell me now. I spared you once. I will not do that again. Tell me what you know about Vernico 5!"

"I don't know anything," you say.

"Part of your brain wants to cooperate, but the other half prevents it. I am going to remove that conflict from you," Bartus says. He throws a switch and a blinding white light quickly slices you down the middle from top to bottom. You're standing there in two living, thinking pieces. Bartus threatens to kill part of you, leaving you a half person forever, but still you can only say that you don't know anything about Vernico. Finally he throws another switch in disgust. This time a blue light passes through you.

Go on to PAGE 63.

"But since you have such a strong interest in head graft experiments," the lab tech says, "I'd like you to try a little experiment of my own."

"Leave me alone!" you shout. "Your experiments have given me enough of a headache already." | "Give me a metal pole and I'll do some experimenting on *myself*," the krolt head snarls.

Then the lab tech forces you into what she calls an exchange chamber.

"All that will happen is that my head will exchange places with yours," she explains. "My head will go on your body next to the krolt's head. And your head will switch to my body."

However, just as the exchange button is pushed, there is a small but unexpected power surge. So the experiment doesn't go exactly as the lab tech planned. When you crawl out of the metal chamber, the krolt's head is gone from your shoulders. It's on the lab tech now!! And you are back to normal again. You run out of the lab as all the captives applaud from their cages.

You live the rest of your life on a secret part of Nova Cruz. You avoid Dr. Enutelle and his lab techs — but cause them as much trouble as you can whenever possible.

THE END

As you're struggling *not* to spring on Enutelle, he shouts at his lab tech, "Reverse this Amprodusian immediately! How dare you perform an experiment *I* have not authorized!"

"Sorry, Doctor. There was a misunderstanding in our communication," the lab tech says.

"Perhaps you'd understand me better with a droigt implant?" Enutelle says with a glare.

"It won't happen again, Doctor," the lab tech says, in a shaking voice. "I'll prepare the reversal immediately."

"Do it, because I have other plans for our young friend," Enutelle says, laughing for the first time.

Go on to PAGE 82.

46

When Glinton is safely launched and on his way to try to make a new life, you rush to find Governor Slone. There's no time to lose when you're dealing with a maniac like Dr. Enutelle and his illegal conspiracy to change people into Willingness Workers.

Governor Slone is surprised to see you. But his reaction to everything you tell him is reassuringly confident, quick, and decisive.

"You're right. Enutelle is a madman. This is just what we came up here to prove. But Vernico isn't safe for you now. We'd better find a place for you to hide," he says.

Slone takes you to another shabby, crude, reject's dwelling module. He puts his data nord on the screen to unlock the door. Then he puts you in an elevator and tells you to go to the 23rd floor.

"The 23rd floor in a one-story building?" you say.

"The building was built horizontally so it wouldn't be noticed from the street," Slone says. "You'll be taken care of there. I'll see you later."

Then the elevator starts to move, but you didn't press the button. There are no buttons!! With a sinking feeling, you realize that Governor Slone has betrayed you —and is probably sending you to your death.

Go on to PAGE 51.

You try to explain how you got stuck with all this black market merchandise, but the police put a small electrode in the back of your neck — and suddenly you can't say a word.

Cuff him, the robot captain says, and they put special shoes on your feet. Every time you take a step in these shoes, you get a small electric shock. The harder you step down, the stronger the shock. You'd probably fry yourself if you tried to run.

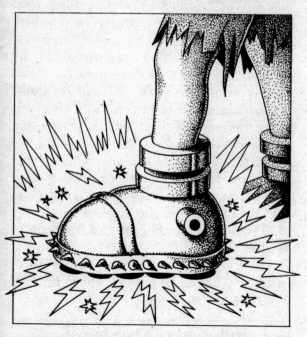

Quick! Tiptoe — fast — to PAGE 92.

48

You open the door to Room 65, and your stomach suddenly transplants itself into your knees. The man sitting on the desk in the office is not Professor Dworkin. It's Dr. Enutelle. He is very short and speaks in a squeaky voice, but it's the way he sits — rigid, not moving a muscle — that convinces you that he really is a man who has rejected all of his human qualities and turned his heart into cold stone.

He speaks to you without moving his head. "You told us you knew nothing about Vernico 5. You convinced almost everyone — except General Bartus. When he rejoined the two halves of your body, he implanted a tracking device so we could follow you. And what did you do then? You disabled one of my best assassins, you embarrassed one of my guards by stealing his jacket, and now you boldly enter my substation. No doubt you are confident that you can do what all these incompetent politicians cannot do — discover my secret for taking over the universe."

"What are you going to do? Talk me to death?" you ask.

The small corners of his mouth twist slightly. That is the only evidence that Dr. Enutelle has smiled at your joke.

If you like animals, turn to PAGE 55.
If you don't, turn to PAGE 72.

BOOOOM!!!

THE END

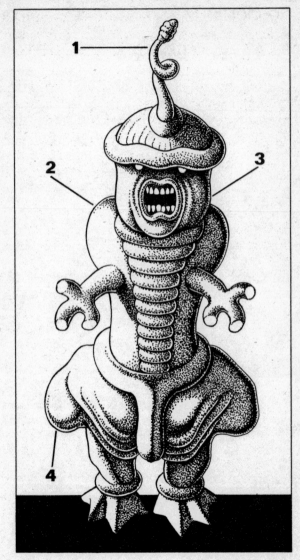

When the elevator slows down, you instinctively move to the farthest corner of the small metal box. The car stops, and the door slides open.

Your welcoming committee is a tall droyfer, an evolutionary oddity that seems very good-natured. The droyfer smiles at you and you feel better. Then the droyfer shoots out an energy shield that turns you upside down. He leads you that way down a long, dark hallway, laughing in his deep ugly voice, "Hu, hu, hu."

The droyfer kicks open a door and throws you on the floor of a small room. Inside the room there are about 50 rejects all waiting in a line. As each reject's turn comes, a second droyfer slips a smooth silver mask over the reject's head. The mask glows for a second and then it is removed. The people don't look hurt. But they don't look happy, either.

"You're next," says your droyfer.

You've got to do something before they put that mask on you. If you know the correct pressure points on a droyfer, you might be able to overpower it. Take a look at the diagram on page 50.

If you think they're 1 and 4, turn to PAGE 6.

If you think they're 2 and 3, turn to PAGE 20.

You run through the streets, hoping to lose yourself in the crowd, but there is no crowd in this corner of Vernico 5. So you've got to get off the walkway and hide somewhere — fast. Just then you see a building with a sign that practically shouts WELCOME to you. It says REJECT GAMES ARCADE. You run straight for it and practically jump through the door.

Inside, the arcade is dimly lit, with low ceilings and a dirt floor. As your eyes adjust to the light, you can make out the forms of about 15 rejects in the place, all wearing their sacklike clothes. Unfortunately, the games they're playing are not the computer-vid games you're used to. Instead, they've got shuffleboard, canasta, ring toss, and pick-up sticks. And a few rejects are crowded around an ancient machine that squeaks and clanks. It's called Donkey Kong.

That's hard enough to take. But then you see the familiar face you were hoping for — not exactly the answer to your prayers. It's a Fourth Unit robot — the one your Aunt Doro uses to drag you to your laser piano lessons!

Go on to PAGE 67.

The head graft operation is a success. But you and your new krolt head hate each other and fight constantly for control of your body.

During the weeks that follow, you are put in charge of an entire section of experimental people and the "things" Enutelle turns them into. Of course, you want to help them. The krolt wants to torture them.

"I don't know how much longer I can go on living like this," you tell your only friend in the lab, a young girl with wolf ears.	"I'd like to tear off both your arms and stuff them in your furry ears" your krolt head tells your only friend.

"Use this on the krolt head," she says, handing you a minisyringe filled with poison. She stole it and was trying to find a way to use it against her captors.

If you want to use the minisyringe on the krolt head, turn to PAGE 37.

If you are afraid of the effect it might have on you, turn to PAGE 57.

"Why do you deal in this junk?" you ask again, hoping the police can still hear.

"I never sell it to anyone who deserves to live," the man explains. "But as for the others — well, if they want it so much that they'll pay the kind of prices I charge, who am I to tell them no?"

You glare at each other.

"Just think of it this way," he tries again. "If I can eliminate one half of all the fools in this world, then the world is a better place to live in by one half."

"Just think of it this way," you say, "you're a greedy murderer."

"Yes, I have made a profit from murder, but yours will be just for the sheer pleasure of it," he says, raising the knife.

Suddenly, the plastic walls around you glow red and then drip down into large wet puddles. The man looks confused for a second. "The police? You little rodent. Well, you will go first," he says politely and flips the switch on the knife. But the weapon never fires. The man is hit with beams of light from all sides. He glows red, then yellow, and a second later he's not standing there. He doesn't exist.

Go on to PAGE 76.

With a horrible laugh, Dr. Enutelle picks you up and throws you into a tiny room. An old man is curled up sleeping at the foot of the room's only bed. It's Professor Dworkin. There are a million questions you want to ask him, but he's sleeping so peacefully you don't want to wake him. Maybe he's dreaming about running away, because his legs kick occasionally.

On a table by a small lamp, there is a stack of pieces of paper — torn napkins and shirt pockets. You quickly realize that these are the pages of the professor's makeshift diary. You begin to read them.

FEBRUARY 28 — *My third day in captivity. Enutelle talks to me freely, explaining his purpose like a child reporting to his father. He is taking over the substation to complete his newest experiment. He learned of this top secret location through his secret partner, G* ——

But the page is torn off there, so you have to read the next one.

MARCH 30 — *Enutelle can make people do whatever he orders. His new treatment destroys their free will when threatened. Subjects become so frightened of being hurt that they will do anything — even something they hate and know is wrong. I must stop him somehow.*

Go on to PAGE 56.

The next diary entry skips a couple of months.

JUNE 7 — *My own experiments in non-material transportation continue, although finding supplies to work with is difficult. I hate this room. It is small and dirty. I'd love to be somewhere where I could run free and climb trees.*

JULY 12 — *I caught a mouse in the room today. It was quite a chase, but I was too sly for it in the end. I played with it for a while before I killed it.*

AUGUST 27 — *Enutelle does not humor me with his visits anymore unless there is a scientific answer he wants to beat out of me. I wouldn't mind scratching his eyes out. I have developed a serious craving for milk.*

AUGUST 45 — *Meow, meow, meow.*

So much for asking the professor a million questions. Maybe if you'd gone to Governor Slone when you had the chance, none of this would have happened. Maybe he could have stopped Enutelle.

Your hopes are at their lowest when Professor Dworkin wakes up and rubs his head against your leg. Nope, he's not going to be much help in stopping Enutelle. But he turns out to be a pretty good lap cat while you wait out eternity in this room.

THE END

You refuse the minisyringe, fearing the poison might go through your system and kill you, too. Instead, you free all of the humans in the lab and ask them to help you force the lab tech to reverse your operation.

"Here she comes!" shouts your friend.

When she sees everyone out of their cages, the lab tech tries to run out, but a human closes and locks the door.

"Get rid of the krolt head. Take it off now!" you demand.

"Exterminate this human vermin once and for all," your krolt head says.

"Get back in your cages before I tighten your collars," the lab tech shouts to the other humans.

"No Problem," they all say as one voice. And they obediently climb back in their cages and lock themselves in.

What happened to your supporters???

"You have just seen a demonstration of Dr. Enutelle's newest creation — the Willingness Worker. Dr. Enutelle will be attempting a large-scale experiment with them soon — very soon," she says.

"What do you consider large-scale?" you ask.

"Is the universe large enough for you?" she says with a bright smile.

Go on to PAGE 44.

You lie down and take deep breaths. Gradually, your heart slows down, your breathing becomes shallow and less frequent, and your body temperature drops. It's an old trick you've known for years, but it just might work. In a room without sound and light, the police must be monitoring you by your life signs. If you don't have any, maybe they'll come to investigate.

Just before you slip into unconsciousness, one wall of the silent dome slides back. Several police robots enter quickly to look for you in the dark. The door is open and now's your chance to run! You fill your lungs with air and take off.

The light in the hall hurts your eyes, but you can't stop to let them adjust. You run, hoping your instincts will lead you in the right direction.

"Stop! You're going the wrong way!" a voice cries from another prisoner's cell. It's a young woman looking out at you through a small window. When you start to run the other way, she says, "Wait! Let me come with you. Please!"

If you want her to come with you, turn to PAGE 81.

If you want to leave her, turn to PAGE 84.

Dr. Enutelle is not easy to track. He ducks down alleyways and turns at nearly every street corner. He pushes his way through a line of rejects waiting for bread. Then something strange happens. Enutelle drops a notebook from under his arm. The rejects ignore it. Don't they see it? Or don't they care?

You care, and once you're certain that Enutelle is out of sight, you make a mad dash for the notebook.

The cover says *Experiments in Altering the Human Will.* It's filled with scientific formulas and energy diagrams. But one page spells out an unbelievable plan to take over the universe.

You look up from the notebook. The line of rejects still stretches in front of you like a wall. But through that wall is Dr. Enutelle, glaring at you and at his notebook. You take off, but suddenly he's in front of you and you run right into him. He raises his arm and you raise yours to protect yourself. Enutelle gently pricks your finger with a gold needle. Two seconds later, you're asleep.

When you wake up, the air feels and smells different, the sounds are different — you must be on another planet.

Go on to PAGE 26.

The black-jacketed guard leads you to an office door in the Science Transport Substation. The sign on the door says ENU-TELLE, so you kick the door open, startling a small man who is eating a cooked rabbit for his dinner.

"Dr. Enutelle, it makes me sick just to look at you. You are an embarrassment to the universe! I know about your Treatment that turns people into Willingness Workers. Only a degenerate, crazed, hateful maniac, or a triple reject, could think of such a thing!" you tell him, shouting at the top of your lungs.

After you give Dr. Enutelle a piece of your mind, he orders General Bartus to *take* a piece of it, permanently. Bartus drags you back to the glass octagonal room, where he gives you another demonstration of how he operates with the white light beam.

Afterward you can't turn a page and chew gum at the same time. So you'd better close this book for now, reader. And, in your condition, put it down very carefully.

THE END

You are once again in the octagonal room with the glass walls. Enutelle says he won't hurt you, but why are your hands tied behind your back?

Bartus holds your head between his thorny blue fingers. "There are a dozen ways I'd like to remove your memory," he says. "But orders are orders. I regret to say that this won't hurt a bit." Then he places a thin strip of fiberplas across your forehead.

You look up at him. "Who are you?" you ask.

"Never mind. My job is done. Go to sleep now. You're going home," the general says. "Perhaps we will meet again someday."

The next day you wake up in your own bed, without a thought of Vernico 5. You go out and spend a normal day.

Later that afternoon, when it's just about time for your laser piano lessons, you duck into a 3-D vid-arcade for a quick game or two. You've got a hot trigger finger today, but suddenly Aunt Doro tries to break in on the frequency. You're in no mood for laser piano lessons today, so you run out of the arcade and hop into a space freighter. It should be a safe place to hide for a while — but it isn't. It takes off five seconds later. Destination: Vernico 6.

THE END

Here's a list of the things you do to keep from going nuts during your five days in the silent dome.

- Walk
- Dance
- Give names to your fingernails
- Think about the sound of one hand clapping
- Qualify for the *Guinness Book of Galactic Records* by singing "One Million Bottles of Beer on the Wall"
- Invent a way to teach word processing to otters
- Play charades
- Think about disgusting sandwiches — raw beef/Jell-O/tomato on nine-grain bread wins!
- Try not to think about disgusting sandwiches
- Play tic-tac-toe with real toes
- Decide that you're really a flashlight . . . uh-oh, maybe these techniques aren't working as well as you thought . . .

Go on to PAGE 13.

Much to your surprise, the blue light molds you back together again. "You're free to go," says Bartus. "You have convinced my superiors you're telling the truth. But *I* don't believe you for a second."

Out on a Vernico street, you walk around in circles for a minute, just because it's such a great feeling to be whole again.

"You look lost," somebody says. He is a human, and one of the biggest you've ever seen. Yet his voice is warm and friendly. "You're not a reject, are you?" he asks.

"I'm here by accident, and I want to go home," you say.

"I don't blame you. This is no place for a good kid like you. Vernico has an awful secret," he says.

"What is it?" you ask.

"I don't know, but my feelings never lie to me," he says. "You're in a lot of trouble, more trouble than you know. My dwelling module is close by. Come. A hot meal will do you good."

Suddenly you see Governor Slone and the others coming from the launch area.

"Don't trust Slone," the reject says. "Not with your life — not on Vernico 5."

If you want to go with the reject, turn to PAGE 7.

If you want to ask Slone for help, turn to PAGE 10.

The space rambler guides like a charm. It's nice to know you have a friend like Ian Slone who can pull some strings now and then.

Vernico 5 is growing smaller behind you. Suddenly, the panel of lights in front of you is flashing like the lights on a Christmas tree. TROUBLE ON THE DOWNSPEED ROCKET. You flip on the vid-camera — and blink in disbelief. Trouble on the downspeed rocket?? There is no downspeed rocket!! It's floating behind you. You're down to half speed and struggling to keep on course.

You're frantically busy pushing buttons and reprogramming on-board computers that don't work anymore, and for a minute or two you ignore what is really going on. Then it hits you. This ship isn't just going on the fritz. It's been rigged to fall apart in space — and kill you!!

Go on to PAGE 89.

You push a few buttons and flip a few switches. Suddenly a mechanical arm reaches out of the control panel and gives you a mug of hot chicken soup. First rule of the galaxy: Nobody should fly on an empty stomach.

So you drink the soup, and afterward you power off. In seconds, you're thousands of miles away from the man who gave you this cargo. And the navigation computer is guiding you swiftly to a predetermined destination. But you're still dying to know what illegal and possibly dangerous cargo you're hauling. So a few minutes later you shut down the power-burn and let the ship coast slowly while you go into the cargo hold to check it out.

You try to kick several of the drums to see if they rattle. Some of them are heavy, others aren't. But they're all sealed tight with an unusual electromagnetic force field. When you touch it, you get a painful shock. And if that isn't enough, stamped on the side of each drum in red ink are the words DO NOT OPEN UNTIL CHRISTMAS.

If you're nosy enough to want to open these drums, turn to PAGE 68.

If you think maybe you'd better not be nosy about this stuff, turn to PAGE 79.

"She is the third," another reject says, slowly taking two pieces of paper from under his burlap shirt.

Two more suicide notes . . .

Today I betrayed my neighbor because a guard threatened to pinch my cheek if I didn't. I believe I have had the Treatment, but I can't remember anything about it. I cannot live with these doubts any longer.

And the other reads simply, *I am too ashamed.*

"I know all about the Willingness Workers," you say. "And I know who is responsible. We can destroy them if we help each other," you say loudly.

"Rejects are forbidden from meeting in groups," a reject reminds you. "There is nothing we can do."

This attitude boils your blood. "I want to see every Willingness Worker with me at Governor Slone's launchpad in half an hour or I'm going to do some head-banging of my own!" you shout fiercely, without planning to.

"No Problem!" all of the Willingness Worker rejects shout back quickly.

Hey, you've started something. Pretty soon the cry goes up all over Vernico: "Governor Slone's launchpad — No Problem! No Problem!!"

Go on to PAGE 86.

The Fourth Unit robot's face plate swivels, and a small screen appears. In a few seconds, your Aunt Doro's face comes on the screen. She smiles, but only for one-and-a half seconds. "I knew we'd find you in one arcade or another," she says. "I have only two words for you: GET HOME!"

That's not going to be so easy, you think to yourself, just as the robot grabs the front of your shirt in its pincer and pulls you out of the arcade.

Outside, a horrible but familiar group is forming a reunion for you. The robot drags you right into the midst of the trio — the enormous human (who is still limping), Dr. Enutelle, and General Bartus. The human takes one giant step forward, but the robot flips out a telescoping arm. It touches the reject, who instantly evaporates into a white cloud. Then the robot's head swivels and sprays General Bartus with something that makes the crayt's feet grow roots in the ground. Dr. Enutelle looks at them, and at the robot, and then at you. "Have a nice trip home," he says politely.

The robot brings you back home and forces you to practice day after day. And it's all for the best because you go on to become a universally (and we mean *universally*) respected laser concert pianist.

THE END

With a rearrangement of the circuit boards in the control panel, you reverse the polarity of your ship. That little trick almost sends you hurtling into subspace, but it breaks the security seal on the drums.

In the first drum you find a year's supply of Choco-Raspberry Lunch Meat. This used to be a very popular lunch treat. Kids loved it because it was sweet. And adults bought it because it had lots of protein. But scientists discovered that if you ate *it*, it ate *you*! After 600 sandwiches of the stuff, your stomach looked like Swiss cheese.

The next drum is worse. It contains Xepon Gas Headlights. They're much brighter than normal, but if they break in a crash, the Xepon gas destroys all plant and small animal life within a 50-mile radius.

You also discover Eardrum Radios, Acid Underwear, Fluorocarbon Flashlights, Brain Wave Blocker Diet Pills, and some well known but completely hideous gag gifts such as 10-Megaton Exploding Cigars and the Laser Joy Buzzer.

All of this junk has two things in common. It's all made on the planet Japponn, and it's all completely illegal.

If you want to dump the drums into space, turn to PAGE 23.

If you want to try Choco-Raspberry Lunch Meat, take a bite on PAGE 71.

"What I don't understand," you say, "is what's going to happen to you guards if he *does* launch the missile? I mean, won't you all become Willingness Workers, too?"

"No," says the guard, "Enutelle told us we'll all hide in the steel vault with him. We'll·be protected from the blast down there and won't get the Treatment."

"Yeah, well I think that's the part that's changed," you say. "Phase 2 calls for the extermination of all guards. The steel vault holds only one person. And who do you think that one person is?"

The guard stops walking. Suddenly he's not in such a hurry to bring you to Enutelle.

"If you think I'm lying, take me to the steel vault and I'll show you," you say.

The guard has never been there, but he knows where the secret elevator is that leads to the vault. You both climb aboard and go 17 miles straight down at a mile a second. And you know what? You guessed right! The steel vault is a tiny little square room with steel walls two feet thick.

"We can't all fit in that!" the guard shouts.

You dash into the steel vault, slamming the door behind you, and throwing the electrovacuum lock.

Go on to PAGE 70.

The steel vault you're in is designed as a very simple home. It has enough food and books to feed one person — body and mind — for three months. It has a radio transmitter. And it has one red button. You don't have to think twice about what that button is for. You immediately get Enutelle on the com-phone.

"In exactly two hours I am pushing this red button," you say. "Dismantle your missile before that."

"I take orders from no one in the universe," Enutelle says.

"If you haven't dismantled your missile, Doctor, you will become a Willingness Worker and my personal slave for the rest of your life. And I promise you'll take more orders than a food tech!" you say.

But at the end of two hours, you aren't sure what you should actually do. If you push the button and the missile hasn't been dismantled, you will turn everyone who exists into Willingness Workers. But if you don't push the button, how will you know for sure that the missile has been dismantled?

Your time is up. You've got to decide . . . now.

If you want to push the button, turn to PAGE 77.

If you don't, turn to PAGE 85.

As you break the seal on a package of Choco-Raspberry Lunch Meat, you think to yourself, *600 sandwiches can kill you, but one little bite can't hurt.* Besides, you've been curious about this stuff for years.

Your first big bite tells you it's everything the package says it is. It's real lunch meat, with 95% of all the proteins and vitamins you could ask for, *and* it tastes exactly like a chocolate-raspberry milkshake.

It's also something else the package says it is — it's out of date. But you didn't look closely enough to see that. The expiration date was two years ago, and the dangerous effects have accelerated 200 times.

Suddenly you don't feel very well. You'd like to take the meat out of your mouth. But you can't. The first thing the stuff does is seal your mouth shut. Then things start getting really strange. Your body starts to change. When it's over, an hour later, you are a tall, stalky, green-and-purple plant packed with vitamins whose leaves smell like a chocolate-raspberry milkshake.

THE END

Dr. Enutelle throws you into a room a few doors down from his office. You pound on the door until your hands throb in pain.

"That won't do any good," an old man's voice says.

You thought you were alone! You wheel around in the direction of the voice, your eyes wide and ready.

"It took me about a year to realize that I would never get out of this room through that door. This discovery helped me focus on the important things in life, such as getting out of here some other way before Dr. Enutelle completes his missile. If he launches it, he will turn everyone in the universe into Willingness Workers. Everyone will be his slave!"

The old man is Professor Dworkin. He continues. "Three years ago, your government sent me to Vernico to work in peace. But someone told Enutelle about the S.T. Substation, and he moved right in to perfect his mind control plot."

The professor, working with scraps in the room and with your assistance, completes his experiments in nonmaterial transportation. And just before Enutelle launches his missile, the professor takes you to another galaxy, where you spend the rest of your life among peaceful, kind people.

THE END

You leap at Enutelle and tear him to pieces in a uniquely Amprodusian display of viciousness. By the time you're done, Enutelle's guards have fled halfway to another galaxy.

You release all of the human guinea pigs and once again point to the word you have written. You plead for their HELP.

By searching through Enutelle's files, the young people discover his notes on the reversal process for Amprodusians. And, surprise! The notes reveal that the other Amprodusian is Keddy Bloom, a tough kid from your home planet. He refuses the reversal process and chooses to stay as he is. You, however, can't wait to look and feel like your old self again.

Fortunately, that takes only a day.

After that, you explore this beautiful planet as your own self. You lie on its beaches and climb its trees. And you never have to take piano lessons again!

THE END

SPACE PILOT'S LICENSE
LEARNER'S PERMIT EXAM

Select the one answer you think is correct in each question. CAUTION: The penalty for cheating is a $500 fine or death for up to six months.

1. You are flying, and you see a space freighter coming toward you in your flight lane. What should you do?
   (a) Ray-blast the chump to space dust.
   (b) Switch to lightspeed, and pass the freighter by a couple of years.
   (c) Expect to be home very, very late.

2. You and three other spaceships are stopped at a four-way space station. Who may launch first?
   (a) The ship that can put the pedal to the metal fastest.
   (b) The ship whose pilot chose 1.(a).
   (c) The ship that doesn't want to be a rotten egg.

3. When is it permissible to make a figure U course shift?
   (a) When your horoscope says it's okay.
   (b) When you've missed the last exit for McRobot's Brownburgers.
   (c) When you're enrolled as a full-time student taking at least 12 credits but no more than 16.

Continue test on PAGE 75.

4. Which sign means *If you can read this sign, you're too close to this planet?*
5. Which sign means *Intergalactic Rest Area Ahead?*
6. Which sign means *Pedestrian Crossing?*
7. Which sign means *No Extraterrestrial Hitchhiking?*

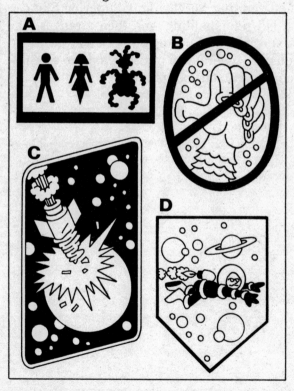

Go on to page 80 to find your score.

Seconds later, the police rush in from everywhere to save you. Although they couldn't capture the man alive, they find his bookkeeping disks and all of the evidence they need to put an end to the smuggling setup.

Later, back at the police satellite, the Intergalactic Council gives you an award for Outstanding Service and Superior Standards/Understanding, and then arranges for a special ship to take you back to your own planet, where you receive a hero's welcome in a starfleet parade.

THE END

You push the button and hope for the best. After a minute, you begin calling on the com-phone, but Enutelle doesn't answer. No one does. Have you turned everyone into Willingness Workers? Have you killed everyone in the universe? Why doesn't someone answer? Finally a voice answers your call.

"This is Governor Elise Monroe of the star district Alpha Trova. You can come up now. Everyone's safe and sound up here, thanks to you," she says.

It's true. Enutelle hated the idea of taking orders from you so much he dismantled his bomb in 30 seconds. Then he spent five minutes jumping up and down on the pieces. However, when you step out of the elevator, Enutelle is nowhere to be found. A secret accomplice has helped him escape from Vernico. Who is it? The governors don't know . . . and you'll never find out until the next time you take the Journey to Vernico 5.

THE END

Unable to force Enutelle to defuse the bomb, the visiting governors summon the Emergency Unit. Enutelle laughs in their faces — until the unit arrives. Suddenly the entire planet is enveloped in a Freeze. Every living person, plant, and alien is put into suspended animation. During the Freeze, the Emergency Unit lands on Vernico 5, removes Enutelle and Slone, and defuses the bomb. The unit operators also consume 24 dinners and 12 dozen doughnuts without paying for them. Then they leave as quickly as they came.

When people start to move again, they thank you for putting an end to Enutelle's Willingness Worker Plot.

Back on your home planet, you are a hero and are decorated in a fabulous ceremony that lasts for a week.

Not bad for a morning's work . . .

THE END

Christmas is a long way off. And you decide you'll see what's in the drums sooner or later — probably when you deliver the merchandise to the Intergalactic Council police. Besides, you've got better things to think about: the rewards and commendations you'll get for breaking up this illegal smuggling racket. You head back for the navigation chamber, trying to decide which is your best side for the vidscreen newspaper photographs.

And guess what? You're right. You *do* find out what's in the drums sooner or later — sooner than you want to. Thirty seconds after you leave the cargo hold, five of the drums explode, turning the spaceship into a jigsaw puzzle of a million pieces. The bombs were supposed to be a big surprise for the real delivery person — someone the smugglers didn't trust anymore. Unfortunately for you, you were simply in the wrong place at the right time — the five bombs didn't know they weren't for you.

Next time, maybe you *should* put your nose where it doesn't belong. At least, that way maybe you'll still have a nose to put.

THE END

You quickly push a couple of wires together in her cell door locking mechanism. There's a spark, then a puff of black smoke, and the door slides open. The young woman steps out of her cell, smiling sweetly at you. She shakes your hand and then screams at the top of her lungs, "Here's the escaped prisoner!!" while holding onto you with a tight grip.

Police are on you in a second. "Good work," they tell the woman prisoner. "We'll remember this when it comes time for parole."

You'll remember it for the rest of your life — which, of course, you spend in jail. After they catch you, the police reason that an innocent person would never try to escape. So you must be guilty. And the computer jury agrees. However, just to show you a little mercy, the police let you have a laser piano in your cell.

THE END

The reversal is a success, but Dr. Enutelle does indeed have other plans for you.

This time he is going to get rid of you for good. He seals you into a veriguard capsule, which he then loads into an ejector.

"Are you shooting me out into space to die?" you ask.

"No, I am not merely sending you off into space. You are going out of my life and over the rainbow — in short, I am sending you back through time," he says. He pushes the button and you are launched. The veriguard capsule disassembles and reassembles your molecules several times and finally you crash-land in your new home.

You are forced to become a citizen of a place called Hollywood, California, on the planet called Earth in the ancient time of the 1980's. And so you make the best of the situation, doing the only thing you know how: making movies about home — outer space. You become a famous movie director, and needless to say, the critics and audiences go wild over the realism and originality of your films.

THE END

You and Glinton hit starspeed and return to your home planet of Nector Alpha. The next week Glinton requests a status review, which turns out positive, especially since Keddy Bloom is so proud of his dirty tricks that he freely admits them. Soon after that, Keddy Bloom is sent to Vernico 5.

Then things return to normal ... until one day three months later. Right in the middle of a star shower one day there is an enormous explosion that rocks the universe. No one seems to know what it is, and then no one seems to remember that it happened. But from then on, whenever anyone threatens you, you (and everyone else in the galaxy) become frightened and say, "No Problem." And you immediately do whatever you are told to do.

And from that day on, your Aunt Doro never has any trouble getting you to practice laser piano again.

THE END

You ignore her and keep on going, but a robot voice behind you calls out, *There's the prisoner!* Now there's no time to lose. You run as fast as you can. But the police must be changing the gravity in the building. Your legs are getting heavier, and it's difficult to lift them to run. If you can make it to the visitors' docking bay ahead of you, you might be able to escape in one of the out-region ships waiting there.

Suddenly you see something that looks really great to you. There's a visitor ship with the emblem of your planet in the dock, and it's ready to take off. So you race for the loading lift and hop in just before the hatch closes.

"What do you want?" asks a surprised copilot.

"A ride home. I'm late for a piano lesson," you say, smiling for the first time in hours.

Just as the rocket fires, the crew member says, "But we're not going home. We're going to Vernico 5."

Go on to PAGE 14.

You're betting that Enutelle will dismantle his Willingness Worker bomb. But Enutelle is betting that your good heart will keep you from pushing the button. He wins the bet.

As soon as you step out of the steel vault, Enutelle and a dozen guards greet you forcibly. Then Enutelle runs into the steel vault, seals the door, and announces that his missile will explode in five minutes.

Panic sweeps through the Science Transport Substation. Everyone tries to escape.

You are forgotten in the chaos, but you can't forget that you had your chance to save the universe and you blew it. You wander outside, a free but sad person.

Suddenly the sky turns black and the air cold. *Is this how it starts?* you wonder. You look up. A gleaming, flashing, *enormous* spaceship — a thousand times bigger than the planet of Vernico! — is slowly descending toward you. The spaceship swallows up Vernico, proving a long-held theory that your entire universe is just a speck of dust in a giant's world.

Seconds later, Enutelle's bomb explodes. But what he thought was the most monstrous plot in history, only gives the occupants of this gigantic spaceship an itch for a week.

THE END

The new Willingness Workers' Army is surrounding Governor Slone's spaceship. And you, along with two of the strongest rejects, storm through the spaceship looking for Slone. You find him in the library, pointing a laser splatter at you.

"Don't take another step," Slone says.

"No Problem," your two rejects say, backing away.

"You can kill *us*, Governor," you say. "But we have your ship surrounded. You'll never get out of here alive, so you'd better give up."

"No Problem, No Problem," the governor says, dropping the weapon instantly. Then he does a double take. "Oh, no — Enutelle has turned me into a Willingness Worker, too!" he says with a bitter sneer. "That double-crossing fiend. He said he was giving me a different treatment so I wouldn't be harmed by the bomb."

"What bomb??!!" everyone else in the room asks.

"The one Enutelle has been building in the Science Transport Substation. It will turn everyone in the universe into Willingness Workers. Then he and I will rule the universe!" the governor says.

Go on to PAGE 18.

As the boy and Clare enter the cage, you back up as far as you can, until you're practically standing on top of the other Amprodusian. They take their time and speak in soft, friendly voices.

When they are more than halfway into the cage, you dart around behind them. Once you are outside the cage, you lock them in. They begin screaming for help from the other young people who are still outside the lab.

The room quickly fills with escaped prisoners, noise, and activity. Too much noise and activity for anyone to notice you at an electronic writing pad on one wall of the lab. But suddenly someone sees.

"There it is!" someone shouts. "Kill it!"

Everyone turns to you and then the group gasps in disbelief. Using every ounce of strength, you have somehow fought off most of your Amprodusian instincts. In a crooked, primitive scrawl, you have written out the word HELP.

Go on to PAGE 16.

Inside, in the unmarked ship's docking area, you see a man approaching. He flips a latch, and the door of your capsule opens.

"I hope you've got big pockets, kid," he says. "I mean, come on, why such a small spaceship? Do you expect to carry this stuff away in your pockets?" As he speaks he gives you a small, friendly slap on the face for emphasis.

"Carry the *stuff* away in my pockets?" you repeat slowly.

"I can't believe my business depends on kids like you. Where'd they find you?" the man says, slapping the side of his own face. "Look, kid. You were waiting in the right place — I thought you'd know the deal," he says. Then he takes you by the shoulders and walks you toward stacks and stacks of large, sealed plastic drums. "I give you the stuff and you deliver it. The buyer gives you a lot of money, which you give to me next week. Is that simple enough for you?"

It's not only simple — it's perfectly clear. Whatever he's selling is illegal. You've got some fast thinking to do. Is this something you want to get involved in?? Is there any way you can *avoid* being involved?

If you play along, turn to PAGE 34.

If you think you'd rather not get involved, turn to PAGE 38.

You've got one chance in a million to live. Every ship this size carries an emergency escape suit. In the suit you could probably last for a few months, at least. Your only hope is that you might be lucky enough to be picked up by another ship.

You suit up and explode the fiery bolts on the emergency hatch. Grasping the ship's umbilical line, you ease out of the ship and prepare for free flight.

The sabotage of your spaceship stinks of Dr. Enutelle and General Bartus. They're probably in it together somehow. You hope that Ian Slone and the other politicians get them for this.

You float in the aloneness of space for what must be several days. Suddenly, an explosion rocks the universe — you know it is the culmination of every horrible dream Enutelle has ever had.

The shock waves of the enormous explosion propel you not just through space, but through time as well. You end up on a planet called Earth in the year 1996. You are Earth's first extraterrestrial! People promise you you'll make a "bundle" by doing something called "talk shows."

THE END

Using mechanical hands and a space scoop, you grab the small object that's floating outside your window and bring it into the capsule.

As you stare at it carefully, a look of wonder and disbelief sweeps across your face. It's impossible but it's *true*! You've found your math homework assignment — the one you told your teacher you lost but she didn't believe you. Talk about being lost in space. Well, now that you've got it back, maybe you won't have to take that whole math tutorial over again. And next time you say you've lost your homework, your teacher better believe you.

THE END

An enormous arm in a black vylar sleeve punches through the light panel and grabs at you. Thinking quickly, you hand her one of the power lines from the lights.

"She'll be unconscious for only a short time," Rory says. "They're programmed to withstand all shocks. Listen — I'm sorry I told her where you were. I couldn't help it. You heard her call me a Willingness Worker. It's something they did to me. They've done it to a lot of rejects. But none of us can remember what it was."

Rory doesn't know how to get into the substation, so you thank him and quickly slip out into the night.

Soon you duck into a dark eating module and sit down. As your eyes become accustomed to the dark you see a guard, sitting by himself, at another table. He has removed his black vylar jacket. You pick up the bottle of steak sauce from your table and toss it into the far corner of the eating module. There are loud screams, and the guard rushes over to investigate.

This is it! The jacket could be your passport past the guards at the S.T. Substation. On the other hand, you might get farther in by giving yourself up.

If you take the jacket, turn to PAGE 31.
If you give yourself up, turn to PAGE 33.

At the police satellite, the robots stuff you into an interrogation room. A guard robot's head swivels back and forth watching as you pace in the little cube. Finally a human detective comes in.

"This is a mistake," you say. "I wasn't supposed to be on that spaceship."

The detective leans over you menacingly. "That's not the answer I want to hear," she says. "Five days in the silent dome for you and then let's have another chat."

You're thrown into the silent dome, an unlighted room with thick padded walls and ceilings. Every sound in the room is completely absorbed. You can't hear yourself move, or breathe, or scream. Five days in here? You'll be lucky if you last five hours.

If you want to try to escape, turn to PAGE 58.

If you don't want to, turn to PAGE 62.

Suddenly your robot partner grabs you by the throat. Its skin feels soft, but you can soon feel the steel under the skin as the robot begins to squeeze.

"You're working for *them*?" you gasp while you still can.

Not even a robot can make ends meet on the salary the police pay. And Mr. Gravestock's smuggling operation pays me well to keep fools like you from messing it up, the robot says.

At least you get a full explanation before you die.

THE END

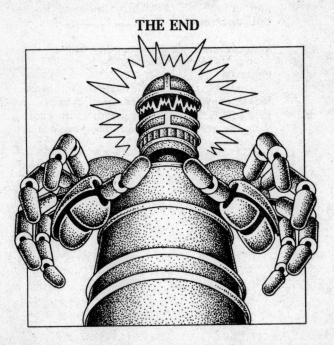

Collect All the Twistaplot® Books
And Choose From Over 200 Endings!

You're lost in the rain. The old house up ahead looks creepy, but maybe someone there can help you. Welcome to Monster Mansion, where vampires, werewolves, and zombies await your arrival.